In
1935 if you wanted to
read a good book, you needed
either a lot of money or a library card.
Cheap paperbacks were available, but their
poor production generally mirrored the quality
between the covers. One weekend that year,
Allen Lane, Managing Director of The Bodley Head,
having spent the weekend visiting Agatha Christie,
found himself on a platform at Exeter station trying to
find something to read for his journey back to London.
He was appalled by the quality of the material he had to
choose from. Everything that Allen Lane achieved from that
day until his death in 1970 was based on a passionate belief
in the existence of 'a vast reading public for *intelligent*
books at a low price'. The result of his momentous vision
was the birth not only of Penguin, but of the 'paperback
revolution'. Quality writing became available for the price of
a packet of cigarettes, literature became a mass medium
for the first time, a nation of book-borrowers became a
nation of book-buyers – and the very concept of book
publishing was changed for ever. Those founding
principles – of quality and value, with an overarching
belief in the fundamental importance of reading –
have guided everything the company has
done since 1935. Sir Allen Lane's
pioneering spirit is still very much alive
at Penguin in 2005. Here's to
the next 70 years!

MORE THAN A BUSINESS

'We decided it was time to end the almost customary half-hearted manner in which cheap editions were produced – as though the only people who could possibly want cheap editions must belong to a lower order of intelligence. We, however, believed in the existence in this country of a vast reading public for intelligent books at a low price, and staked everything on it'
Sir Allen Lane, 1902–1970

'The Penguin Books are splendid value for sixpence, so splendid that if other publishers had any sense they would combine against them and suppress them'
George Orwell

'More than a business … a national cultural asset'
Guardian

'When you look at the whole Penguin achievement you know that it constitutes, in action, one of the more democratic successes of our recent social history'
Richard Hoggart

The Mirror of Ink

JORGE LUIS BORGES

PENGUIN BOOKS

PENGUIN BOOKS

Published by the Penguin Group
Penguin Books Ltd, 80 Strand, London WC2R ORL, England
Penguin Group (USA) Inc., 375 Hudson Street, New York, New York 10014, USA
Penguin Group (Canada), 10 Alcorn Avenue, Toronto, Ontario, Canada M4V 3B2
(a division of Pearson Penguin Canada Inc.)
Penguin Ireland, 25 St Stephen's Green, Dublin 2, Ireland
(a division of Penguin Books Ltd)
Penguin Group (Australia), 250 Camberwell Road, Camberwell, Victoria 3124,
Australia (a division of Pearson Australia Group Pty Ltd)
Penguin Books India Pvt Ltd, 11 Community Centre,
Panchsheel Park, New Delhi – 110 017, India
Penguin Group (NZ), cnr Airborne and Rosedale Roads, Albany,
Auckland 1310, New Zealand (a division of Pearson New Zealand Ltd)
Penguin Books (South Africa) (Pty) Ltd, 24 Sturdee Avenue,
Rosebank 2196, South Africa

Penguin Books Ltd, Registered Offices: 80 Strand, London WC2R ORL, England

www.penguin.com

These translations first published in the USA as *Collected Fictions*
by Viking Penguin, a member of Penguin Putnam Inc. 1998
First published in Penguin Books 1999
This selection published as a Pocket Penguin 2005

1

Copyright © Maria Kodama, 1998
Translations copyright © Penguin Putnam Inc., 1998
All rights reserved

The moral right of the copyright holders has been asserted

Set in 11/13pt Monotype Dante
Typeset by Palimpsest Book Production Limited
Polmont, Stirlingshire
Printed in England by Clays Ltd, St Ives plc

Contents

CHAPTER V

The Mirror of Ink

History records that the cruelest of the governors of the Sudan was Yāqub the Afflicted, who abandoned his nation to the iniquities of Egyptian tax collectors and died in a chamber of the palace on the fourteenth day of the moon of Barmajat in the year 1842. There are those who insinuate that the sorcerer Abderramen al-Masmudī (whose name might be translated 'The Servant of Mercy') murdered him with a dagger or with poison, but a natural death is more likely – especially as he was known as 'the Afflicted.' Nonetheless, Capt. Richard Francis Burton spoke with this sorcerer in 1853, and he reported that the sorcerer told him this story that I shall reproduce here:

'It is true that I suffered captivity in the fortress of Yakub the Afflicted, due to the conspiracy forged by my brother Ibrahim, with the vain and perfidious aid of the black chieftains of Kordofan, who betrayed him. My brother perished by the sword upon the bloody pelt of justice, but I threw myself at the abominated feet of the Afflicted One and told him I was a sorcerer, and that if he granted me my life I would show him forms and appearances more marvellous than those of the *fanusi jihal*, the magic lantern. The tyrant demanded an immediate proof;

I called for a reed pen, a pair of scissors, a large sheet of Venetian paper, an inkhorn, a chafing-dish with live charcoal in it, a few coriander seeds, and an ounce of benzoin. I cut the paper into six strips and wrote charms and invocations upon the first five; on the last I inscribed the following words from the glorious Qur'ān: "We have removed from thee thy veil, and thy sight is piercing." Then I drew a magic square in Yakub's right palm and asked him to hold it out to me; into it, I poured a circle of ink. I asked him whether he could see his face in the circle, and he told me that he could see it clearly. I instructed him not to raise his eyes. I put the benzoin and the coriander seeds into the chafing-dish and therein also burned the invocations. I asked the Afflicted One to name the figure that he wished to see. He thought for a moment and told me that he wished to see a wild horse, the most beautiful creature that grazed upon the meadows that lie along the desert. He looked, and he saw first green and peaceful fields and then a horse coming toward him, as graceful as a leopard and with a white star upon its forehead. He then asked me for a herd of such horses, as perfect as the first, and he saw upon the horizon a long cloud of dust, and then the herd. I sensed that my life was safe.

'Hardly had the sun appeared above the horizon when two soldiers entered my cell and conveyed me to the chamber of the Afflicted One, wherein I found awaiting me the incense, the chafing-dish, and the ink. Thus day by day did he make demands upon my skill, and thus day by day did I show to him the appearances of

2

this world. That dead man whom I abominate held within his hand all that dead men have seen and all that living men see: the cities, climes, and kingdoms into which this world is divided, the hidden treasures of its center, the ships that sail its seas, its instruments of war and music and surgery, its graceful women, its fixed stars and the planets, the colors taken up by the infidel to paint his abominable images, its minerals and plants with the secrets and virtues which they hold, the angels of silver whose nutriment is our praise and justification of the Lord, the passing-out of prizes in its schools, the statues of birds and kings that lie within the heart of its pyramids, the shadow thrown by the bull upon whose shoulders this world is upheld, and by the fish below the bull, the deserts of Allah the Merciful. He beheld things impossible to describe, such as streets illuminated by gaslight and such as the whale that dies when it hears man's voice. Once he commanded me to show him the city men call Europe. I showed him the grandest of its streets and I believe that it was in that rushing flood of men, all dressed in black and many wearing spectacles, that he saw for the first time the Masked One.

'From that time forth, that figure, sometimes in the dress of the Sudanese, sometimes in uniform, but ever with a veil upon its face, crept always into the visions. Though it was never absent, we could not surmise who it might be. And yet the appearances within the mirror of ink, at first momentary or unmoving, became now more complex; they would unhesitatingly obey my commands, and the tyrant could clearly follow them.

In these occupations, both of us, it is true, sometimes became exhausted. The abominable nature of the scenes was another cause of weariness; there was nothing but tortures, garrotes, mutilations, the pleasures of the executioner and the cruel man.

'Thus did we come to the morning of the fourteenth day of the moon of Barmajat. The circle of ink had been poured into the palm, the benzoin sprinkled into the chafing-dish, the invocations burned. The two of us were alone. The Afflicted One commanded me to show him a just and irrevocable punishment, for that day his heart craved to see a death. I showed him soldiers with tambours, the stretched hide of a calf, the persons fortunate enough to look on, the executioner with the sword of justice. The Afflicted One marvelled to see this, and said to me: *It is Abu Kir, the man that slew thy brother Ibrahim, the man that will close thy life when I am able to command the knowledge to convoke these figures without thy aid.* He asked me to bring forth the condemned man, yet when he was brought forth the Afflicted One grew still, because it was the enigmatic man that kept the white cloth always before his visage. The Afflicted One commanded me that before the man was killed, his mask should be stripped from him. I threw myself at his feet and said: *O king of time and substance and peer-less essence of the century, this figure is not like the others, for we know not his name nor that of his fathers nor that of the city which is his homeland. Therefore, O king, I dare not touch him, for fear of committing a sin for which I shall be held accountable.* The Afflicted One laughed and swore that he himself would bear the responsibility for the sin, if sin it was. He swore this by his sword and by the Qur'ān. Then it was that I commanded that the condemned man be stripped naked and bound to the stretched hide of the calf and his mask removed from him. Those things were accomplished; the horrified eyes of Yakub at last saw the visage – which was his own face. In fear and madness, he hid his eyes. I held in my firm right hand his trembling hand and commanded him to look upon the ceremony of his death. He was possessed by the mirror; he did not even try to turn his eyes aside, or to spill out the ink. When in the vision the sword fell upon the guilty neck, he moaned and cried out in a voice that inspired no pity in me, and fell to the floor, dead.

'Glory to Him Who does not die, and Who holds within His hand the two keys, of infinite Pardon and infinite Punishment.'

From Richard Francis Burton,
The Lake Regions of Equatorial Africa

The Lottery in Babylon

Like all the men of Babylon, I have been proconsul; like all, I have been a slave. I have known omnipotence, ignominy, imprisonment. Look here – my right hand has no index finger. Look here – through this gash in my cape you can see on my stomach a crimson tattoo – it is the second letter, *Beth*. On nights when the moon is full, this symbol gives me power over men with the mark of Gimel, but it subjects me to those with the Aleph, who on nights when there is no moon owe obedience to those marked with the Gimel. In the half-light of dawn, in a cellar, standing before a black altar, I have slit the throats of sacred bulls. Once, for an entire lunar year, I was declared invisible – I would cry out and no one would heed my call, I would steal bread and not be beheaded. I have known that thing the Greeks knew not – uncertainty. In a chamber of brass, as I faced the strangler's silent scarf, hope did not abandon me; in the river of delights, panic has not failed me. Heraclides Ponticus reports, admiringly, that Pythagoras recalled having been Pyrrhus, and before that, Euphorbus, and before that, some other mortal; in order to recall similar vicissitudes, I have no need of death, nor even of imposture.

I owe that almost monstrous variety to an institution

– the Lottery – which is unknown in other nations, or
at work in them imperfectly or secretly. I have not delved
into this institution's history. I know that sages cannot
agree. About its mighty purposes I know as much as a
man untutored in astrology might know about the
moon. Mine is a dizzying country in which the Lottery
is a major element of reality; until this day, I have
thought as little about it as about the conduct of the
indecipherable gods or of my heart. Now, far from
Babylon and its beloved customs, I think with some
bewilderment about the Lottery, and about the blasphemous conjectures that shrouded men whisper in the
half-light of dawn or evening.

My father would tell how once, long ago – centuries?
years? – the lottery in Babylon was a game played by
commoners. He would tell (though whether this is true
or not, I cannot say) how barbers would take a man's
copper coins and give back rectangles made of bone or
parchment and adorned with symbols. Then, in broad
daylight, a drawing would be held; those smiled upon
by fate would, with no further corroboration by chance,
win coins minted of silver. The procedure, as you can
see, was rudimentary.

Naturally, those so-called 'lotteries' were a failure.
They had no moral force whatsoever; they appealed not
to all a man's faculties, but only to his hopefulness.
Public indifference soon meant that the merchants who
had founded these venal lotteries began to lose money.
Someone tried something new: including among the list
of lucky numbers a few *unlucky* draws. This innovation

meant that those who bought those numbered rectangles now had a twofold chance: they might win a
sum of money or they might be required to pay a fine
– sometimes a considerable one. As one might expect,
that small risk (for every thirty 'good' numbers there
was one ill-omened one) piqued the public's interest.
Babylonians flocked to buy tickets. The man who
bought none was considered a pusillanimous wretch, a
man with no spirit of adventure. In time, this justified
contempt found a second target: not just the man who
didn't play, but also the man who lost and paid the fine.
The Company (as it was now beginning to be known)
had to protect the interest of the winners, who could
not be paid their prizes unless the pot contained almost
the entire amount of the fines. A lawsuit was filed
against the losers: the judge sentenced them to pay the
original fine, plus court costs, or spend a number of
days in jail. In order to thwart the Company, they all
chose jail. From that gauntlet thrown down by a few
men sprang the Company's omnipotence – its ecclesi-
astical, metaphysical force.

Some time after this, the announcements of the
numbers drawn began to leave out the lists of fines and
simply print the days of prison assigned to each losing
number. That shorthand, as it were, which went virtually
unnoticed at the time, was of utmost importance: *It was
the first appearance of nonpecuniary elements in the lottery*.
And it met with great success – indeed, the Company was
forced by its players to increase the number of unlucky
draws.

As everyone knows, the people of Babylon are great admirers of logic, and even of symmetry. It was inconsistent that lucky numbers should pay off in round silver coins while unlucky ones were measured in days and nights of jail. Certain moralists argued that the possession of coins did not always bring about happiness, and that other forms of happiness were perhaps more direct.

The lower-caste neighborhoods of the city voiced a different complaint. The members of the priestly class gambled heavily, and so enjoyed all the vicissitudes of terror and hope; the poor (with understandable, or inevitable, envy) saw themselves denied access to that famously delightful, even sensual, wheel. The fair and reasonable desire that all men and women, rich and poor, be able to take part equally in the Lottery inspired indignant demonstrations – the memory of which, time has failed to dim. Some stubborn souls could not (or pretended they could not) understand that this was a *novus ordo seclorum*, a necessary stage of history. . . . A slave stole a crimson ticket; the drawing determined that that ticket entitled the bearer to have his tongue burned out. The code of law provided the same sentence for stealing a lottery ticket. Some Babylonians argued that the slave deserved the burning iron for being a thief; others, more magnanimous, that the executioner should employ the iron because thus fate had decreed. . . . There were disturbances, there were regrettable instances of bloodshed, but the masses of Babylon at last, over the opposition of the well-to-do, imposed their will; they saw their generous objectives fully achieved. First, the

Company was forced to assume all public power. (The unification was necessary because of the vastness and complexity of the new operations.) Second, the Lottery was made secret, free of charge, and open to all. The mercenary sale of lots was abolished; once initiated into the mysteries of Baal, every free citizen automatically took part in the sacred drawings, which were held in the labyrinths of the god every sixty nights and determined each citizen's destiny until the next drawing. The consequences were incalculable. A lucky draw might bring about a man's elevation to the council of the magi or the imprisonment of his enemy (secret, or known by all to be so), or might allow him to find, in the peaceful dimness of his room, the woman who would begin to disturb him, or whom he had never hoped to see again; an unlucky draw: mutilation, dishonor of many kinds, death itself. Sometimes a single event – the murder of C in a tavern, B's mysterious apotheosis – would be the inspired outcome of thirty or forty drawings. Combining bets was difficult, but we must recall that the individuals of the Company were (and still are) all-powerful, and clever. In many cases, the knowledge that certain happy turns were the simple result of chance would have lessened the force of those outcomes; to forestall that problem, agents of the Company employed suggestion, or even magic. The paths they followed, the intrigues they wove, were invariably secret. To penetrate the innermost hopes and innermost fears of every man, they called upon astrologers and spies. There were certain stone lions, a sacred latrine called Qaphqa, some cracks in a dusty aqueduct – these places, it was generally believed, *gave access to the Company*, and well- or ill-wishing persons would deposit confidential reports in them. An alphabetical file held those *dossiers* of varying veracity.

Incredibly, there was talk of favoritism, of corruption. With its customary discretion, the Company did not reply directly; instead, it scrawled its brief argument in the rubble of a mask factory. This *apologia* is now numbered among the sacred Scriptures. It pointed out, doctrinally, that the Lottery is an interpolation of chance into the order of the universe, and observed that to accept errors is to strengthen chance, not contravene it. It also noted that those lions, that sacred squatting-place, though not disavowed by the Company (which reserved the right to consult them), functioned with no official guarantee.

This statement quieted the public's concerns. But it also produced other effects perhaps unforeseen by its author. It profoundly altered both the spirit and the operations of the Company. I have but little time remaining; we are told that the ship is about to sail – but I will try to explain.

However unlikely it may seem, no one, until that time, had attempted to produce a general theory of gaming. Babylonians are not a speculative people; they obey the dictates of chance, surrender their lives, their hopes, their nameless terror to it, but it never occurs to them to delve into its labyrinthine laws or the revolving spheres that manifest its workings. Nonetheless, the semiofficial statement that I mentioned inspired numerous debates of a legal and mathematical nature. From one of them, there emerged the following conjecture: If the Lottery is an intensification of chance, a periodic infusion of chaos into the cosmos, then is it not appropriate that chance intervene in *every* aspect of the drawing, not just one? Is it not ludicrous that chance should dictate a person's death while the circumstances of that death – whether private or public, whether drawn out for an hour or a century – should *not* be subject to chance? Those perfectly reasonable objections finally prompted sweeping reform; the complexities of the new system (complicated further by its having been in practice for centuries) are understood by only a handful of specialists, though I will attempt to summarize them, even if only symbolically.

Let us imagine a first drawing, which condemns an individual to death. In pursuance of that decree, another drawing is held; out of that second drawing come, say, nine possible executors. Of those nine, four might initiate a third drawing to determine the name of the executioner, two might replace the unlucky draw with a lucky one (the discovery of a treasure, say), another might decide that the death should be exacerbated (death with dishonor, that is, or with the refinement of torture), others might simply refuse to carry out the sentence. . . . That is the scheme of the Lottery, put symbolically. *In reality, the number of drawings is infinite*. No decision is final; all branch into others. The ignorant assume that infinite drawings require infinite time; actually, all that is required is that time be infinitely subdivisible, as in the famous parable of the Race with the Tortoise. That infinitude coincides remarkably well with the sinuous numbers of Chance and with the Heavenly Archetype of the Lottery beloved of Platonists. . . . Some distorted echo of our custom seems to have reached the Tiber: In his *Life of Antoninus Heliogabalus*, Ælius Lampridius tells us that the emperor wrote out on seashells the fate that he intended for his guests at dinner – some would receive ten pounds of gold; others, ten houseflies, ten dormice, ten bears. It is fair to recall that Heliogabalus was raised in Asia Minor, among the priests of his eponymous god.

There are also *impersonal* drawings, whose purpose is unclear. One drawing decrees that a sapphire from Taprobana be thrown into the waters of the Euphrates; another, that a bird be released from the top of a certain tower; another, that every hundred years a grain of sand be added to (or taken from) the countless grains of sand on a certain beach. Sometimes, the consequences are terrible.

Under the Company's beneficent influence, our customs are now steeped in chance. The purchaser of a dozen amphoræ of Damascene wine will not be surprised if one contains a talisman, or a viper; the scribe who writes out a contract never fails to include some error; I myself, in this hurried statement, have misrepresented some splendor, some atrocity – perhaps, too, some mysterious monotony. . . . Our historians, the most perspicacious on the planet, have invented a method for correcting chance; it is well known that the

outcomes of this method are (in general) trustworthy
– although, of course, they are never divulged without
a measure of deception. Besides, there is nothing so
tainted with fiction as the history of the Company. . . .
A paleographic document, unearthed at a certain
temple, may come from yesterday's drawing or from a
drawing that took place centuries ago. No book is
published without some discrepancy between each of
the edition's copies. Scribes take a secret oath to omit,
interpolate, alter. *Indirect* falsehood is also practiced.

The Company, with godlike modesty, shuns all publi-
city. Its agents, of course, are secret; the orders it constantly
(perhaps continually) imparts are no different from those
spread wholesale by impostors. Besides – who will boast
of being a mere impostor? The drunken man who blurts
out an absurd command, the sleeping man who suddenly
awakes and turns and chokes to death the woman sleeping at his side – are they not, perhaps, implementing
one of the Company's secret decisions? That silent func-
tioning, like God's, inspires all manner of conjectures.
One scurrilously suggests that the Company ceased to
exist hundreds of years ago, and that the sacred disorder of our lives is purely hereditary, traditional; another
believes that the Company is eternal, and that it shall
endure until the last night, when the last god shall anni-
hilate the earth. Yet another declares that the Company
is omnipotent, but affects only small things: the cry of
a bird, the shades of rust and dust, the half dreams that
come at dawn. Another, whispered by masked heresi-
archs, says that *the Company has never existed, and never*

will. Another, no less despicable, argues that it makes no difference whether one affirms or denies the reality of the shadowy corporation, because Babylon is nothing but an infinite game of chance.

The Library of Babel

By this art you may contemplate the
variation of the 23 letters . . .

Anatomy of Melancholy, Pt. 2, Sec. II, Mem. IV

The universe (which others call the Library) is composed of an indefinite, perhaps infinite number of hexagonal galleries. In the center of each gallery is a ventilation shaft, bounded by a low railing. From any hexagon one can see the floors above and below – one after another, endlessly. The arrangement of the galleries is always the same: Twenty bookshelves, five to each side, line four of the hexagon's six sides; the height of the bookshelves, floor to ceiling, is hardly greater than the height of a normal librarian. One of the hexagon's free sides opens onto a narrow sort of vestibule, which in turn opens onto another gallery, identical to the first – identical in fact to all. To the left and right of the vestibule are two tiny compartments. One is for sleeping, upright; the other, for satisfying one's physical necessities. Through this space, too, there passes a spiral staircase, which winds upward and downward into the remotest distance. In the vestibule there is a mirror, which faithfully duplicates appearances. Men often infer from this mirror that the Library is not infinite – if it were, what need would there be for that illusory replication? I prefer to dream that burnished surfaces are a figuration and promise of the infinite. . . . Light is provided by certain spherical fruits that bear the name 'bulbs.' There are two of these bulbs in each hexagon, set crosswise. The light they give is insufficient, and unceasing.

Like all the men of the Library, in my younger days I traveled; I have journeyed in quest of a book, perhaps the catalog of catalogs. Now that my eyes can hardly make out what I myself have written, I am preparing to die, a few leagues from the hexagon where I was born. When I am dead, compassionate hands will throw me over the railing; my tomb will be the unfathomable air, my body will sink for ages, and will decay and dissolve in the wind engendered by my fall, which shall be infinite. I declare that the Library is endless. Idealists argue that the hexagonal rooms are the necessary shape of absolute space, or at least of our *perception* of space. They argue that a triangular or pentagonal chamber is inconceivable. (Mystics claim that their ecstasies reveal to them a circular chamber containing an enormous circular book with a continuous spine that goes completely around the walls. But their testimony is suspect, their words obscure. That cyclical book is God.) Let it suffice for the moment that I repeat the classic dictum: *The Library is a sphere whose exact center is any hexagon and whose circumference is unattainable.*

Each wall of each hexagon is furnished with five bookshelves; each bookshelf holds thirty-two books identical in format; each book contains four hundred ten pages; each page, forty lines; each line, approximately eighty black letters. There are also letters on the front cover of each book; those letters neither indicate nor prefigure what the pages inside will say. I am aware that that lack of correspondence once struck men as mysterious. Before summarizing the solution of the mystery (whose discovery, in spite of its tragic consequences, is perhaps the most important event in all history), I wish to recall a few axioms.

First: *The Library has existed* ab æternitate. That truth, whose immediate corollary is the future eternity of the world, no rational mind can doubt. Man, the imperfect librarian, may be the work of chance or of malevolent demiurges; the universe, with its elegant appointments – its bookshelves, its enigmatic books, its indefatigable staircases for the traveler, and its water closets for the seated librarian – can only be the handiwork of a god. In order to grasp the distance that separates the human and the divine, one has only to compare these crude trembling symbols which my fallible hand scrawls on the cover of a book with the organic letters inside – neat, delicate, deep black, and inimitably symmetrical.

Second: *There are twenty-five orthographic symbols.**
That discovery enabled mankind, three hundred years

---

* The original manuscript has neither numbers nor capital letters; punctuation is limited to the comma and the period. Those two marks, the space, and the twenty-two letters of the alphabet are the twenty-five sufficient symbols that our unknown author is referring to. [Ed. note.]

ago, to formulate a general theory of the Library and thereby satisfactorily solve the riddle that no conjecture had been able to divine – the formless and chaotic nature of virtually all books. One book, which my father once saw in a hexagon in circuit 15–94, consisted of the letters M C V perversely repeated from the first line to the last. Another (much consulted in this zone) is a mere labyrinth of letters whose penultimate page contains the phrase *O Time thy pyramids*. This much is known: For every rational line or forthright statement there are leagues of senseless cacophony, verbal nonsense, and incoherency. (I know of one semibarbarous zone whose librarians repudiate the 'vain and superstitious habit' of trying to find sense in books, equating such a quest with attempting to find meaning in dreams or in the chaotic lines of the palm of one's hand. . . . They will acknowledge that the inventors of writing imitated the twenty-five natural symbols, but contend that that adoption was fortuitous, coincidental, and that books in themselves have no meaning. That argument, as we shall see, is not entirely fallacious.)

For many years it was believed that those impenetrable books were in ancient or far-distant languages. It is true that the most ancient peoples, the first librarians, employed a language quite different from the one we speak today; it is true that a few miles to the right, our language devolves into dialect and that ninety floors above, it becomes incomprehensible. All of that, I repeat, is true – but four hundred ten pages of unvarying M C V's cannot belong to any language, however dialectal or primitive it may be. Some have suggested that each letter influences the next, and that the value of M C V on page 71, line 3, is not the value of the same series on another line of another page, but that vague thesis has not met with any great acceptance. Others have mentioned the possibility of codes; that conjecture has been universally accepted, though not in the sense in which its originators formulated it.

Some five hundred years ago, the chief of one of the upper hexagons* came across a book as jumbled as all the others, but containing almost two pages of homogeneous lines. He showed his find to a traveling decipherer, who told him that the lines were written in Portuguese; others said it was Yiddish. Within the century experts had determined what the language actually was: a Samoyed-Lithuanian dialect of Guaraní, with inflections from classical Arabic. The content was also determined: the rudiments of combinatory analysis, illustrated with examples of endlessly repeating variations. Those examples allowed a librarian of genius to discover the fundamental law of the Library. This philosopher observed that all books, however different from one another they might be, consist of identical elements: the space, the period, the comma, and the twenty-two letters of the alphabet. He also posited a

---

* In earlier times, there was one man for every three hexagons. Suicide and diseases of the lung have played havoc with that proportion. An unspeakably melancholy memory: I have sometimes traveled for nights on end, down corridors and polished staircases, without coming across a single librarian.

fact which all travelers have since confirmed: *In all the Library, there are no two identical books.* From those incontrovertible premises, the librarian deduced that the Library is 'total' – perfect, complete, and whole – and that its bookshelves contain all possible combinations of the twenty-two orthographic symbols (a number which, though unimaginably vast, is not infinite) – that is, all that is able to be expressed, in every language. *All* – the detailed history of the future, the autobiographies of the archangels, the faithful catalog of the Library, thousands and thousands of false catalogs, the proof of the falsity of those false catalogs, a proof of the falsity of the *true* catalog, the gnostic gospel of Basilides, the commentary upon that gospel, the commentary on the commentary on that gospel, the true story of your death, the translation of every book into every language, the interpolations of every book into all books, the treatise Bede could have written (but did not) on the mythology of the Saxon people, the lost books of Tacitus.

When it was announced that the Library contained all books, the first reaction was unbounded joy. All men felt themselves the possessors of an intact and secret treasure. There was no personal problem, no world problem, whose eloquent solution did not exist – somewhere in some hexagon. The universe was justified; the universe suddenly became congruent with the unlimited width and breadth of humankind's hope. At that period there was much talk of The Vindications – books of *apologiæ* and prophecies that would vindicate for all time the actions of every person in the universe and that held wondrous arcana for men's futures. Thousands of greedy individuals abandoned their sweet native hexagons and rushed downstairs, upstairs, spurred by the vain desire to find their Vindication. These pilgrims squabbled in the narrow corridors, muttered dark imprecations, strangled one another on the divine staircases, threw deceiving volumes down ventilation shafts, were themselves hurled to their deaths by men of distant regions. Others went insane. . . . The Vindications do exist (I have seen two of them, which refer to persons in the future, persons perhaps not imaginary), but those who went in quest of them failed to recall that the chance of a man's finding his own Vindication, or some perfidious version of his own, can be calculated to be zero.

At that same period there was also hope that the fundamental mysteries of mankind – the origin of the Library and of time – might be revealed. In all likelihood those profound mysteries can indeed be explained in words; if the language of the philosophers is not sufficient, then the multiform Library must surely have produced the extraordinary language that is required, together with the words and grammar of that language. For four centuries, men have been scouring the hexagons. . . . There are official searchers, the 'inquisitors.' I have seen them about their tasks: they arrive exhausted at some hexagon, they talk about a staircase that nearly killed them – some steps were missing – they speak with the librarian about galleries and staircases, and, once in a while, they take up the nearest book and leaf through it, searching for disgraceful or dishonorable words. Clearly, no one expects to discover anything.

That unbridled hopefulness was succeeded, naturally enough, by a similarly disproportionate depression. The certainty that some bookshelf in some hexagon contained precious books, yet that those precious books were forever out of reach, was almost unbearable. One blasphemous sect proposed that the searches be discontinued and that all men shuffle letters and symbols until those canonical books, through some improbable stroke of chance, had been constructed. The authorities were forced to issue strict orders. The sect disappeared, but in my childhood I have seen old men who for long periods would hide in the latrines with metal disks and a forbidden dice cup, feebly mimicking the divine disorder.

Others, going about it in the opposite way, thought the first thing to do was eliminate all worthless books. They would invade the hexagons, show credentials that were not always false, leaf disgustedly through a volume, and condemn entire walls of books. It is to their hygienic, ascetic rage that we lay the senseless loss of millions of volumes. Their name is execrated today, but those who grieve over the 'treasures' destroyed in that frenzy overlook two widely acknowledged facts: One, that the Library is so huge that any reduction by human hands must be infinitesimal. And two, that each book is unique and irreplaceable, but (since the Library is total) there are always several hundred thousand imperfect facsimiles – books that differ by no more than a single letter, or a comma. Despite general opinion, I daresay that the consequences of the depredations committed by the Purifiers have been exaggerated by the horror those same fanatics inspired. They were spurred on by the holy zeal to reach – someday, through unrelenting effort – the books of the Crimson Hexagon – books smaller than natural books, books omnipotent, illustrated, and magical.

We also have knowledge of another superstition from that period: belief in what was termed the Book-Man. On some shelf in some hexagon, it was argued, there must exist a book that is the cipher and perfect compendium *of all other books*, and some librarian must have examined that book; this librarian is analogous to a god. In the language of this zone there are still vestiges of the sect that worshiped that distant librarian. Many have gone in search of Him. For a hundred years, men beat every possible path – and every path in vain. How was one to locate the idolized secret hexagon that sheltered Him? Someone proposed searching by regression: To locate book A, first consult book B, which tells where book A can be found; to locate book B, first consult book C, and so on, to infinity. . . . It is in ventures such as these that I have squandered and spent my years. I cannot think it unlikely that there is such a total book*

---

* I repeat: In order for a book to exist, it is sufficient that it be *possible*. Only the impossible is excluded. For example, no book is also a staircase, though there are no doubt books that discuss and deny and prove that possibility, and others whose structure corresponds to that of a staircase.

on some shelf in the universe. I pray to the unknown gods that some man – even a single man, tens of centuries ago – has perused and read that book. If the honor and wisdom and joy of such a reading are not to be my own, then let them be for others. Let heaven exist, though my own place be in hell. Let me be tortured and battered and annihilated, but let there be one instant, one creature, wherein thy enormous Library may find its justification.

Infidels claim that the rule in the Library is not 'sense,' but 'non-sense,' and that 'rationality' (even humble, pure coherence) is an almost miraculous exception. They speak, I know, of 'the feverish Library, whose random volumes constantly threaten to transmogrify into others, so that they affirm all things, deny all things, and confound and confuse all things, like some mad and hallucinating deity.' Those words, which not only proclaim disorder but exemplify it as well, prove, as all can see, the infidels' deplorable taste and desperate ignorance. For while the Library contains all verbal structures, all the variations allowed by the twenty-five orthographic symbols, it includes not a single absolute piece of nonsense. It would be pointless to observe that the finest volume of all the many hexagons that I myself administer is titled *Combed Thunder*, while another is titled *The Plaster Cramp*, and another, *Axaxaxas mlö*. Those phrases, at first apparently incoherent, are undoubtedly susceptible to cryptographic or allegorical 'reading'; that reading, that justification of the words' order and existence, is itself verbal and, *ex hypothesi*, already contained somewhere in the Library. There is no combination of characters one can make – *dhcmrlchtdj*, for example – that the divine Library has not foreseen and that in one or more of its secret tongues does not hide a terrible significance. There is no syllable one can speak that is not filled with tenderness and terror, that is not, in one of those languages, the mighty name of a god. To speak is to commit tautologies. This pointless, verbose epistle already exists in one of the thirty volumes of the five bookshelves in one of the countless hexagons – as does its refutation. (A number *n* of the possible languages employ the same vocabulary; in some of them, the *symbol* 'library' possesses the correct definition 'everlasting, ubiquitous system of hexagonal galleries,' while a library – the thing – is a loaf of bread or a pyramid or something else, and the six words that define it themselves have other definitions. You who read me – are you certain you understand my language?)

Methodical composition distracts me from the present condition of humanity. The certainty that everything has already been written annuls us, or renders us phantasmal. I know districts in which the young people prostrate themselves before books and like savages kiss their pages, though they cannot read a letter. Epidemics, heretical discords, pilgrimages that inevitably degenerate into brigandage have decimated the population. I believe I mentioned the suicides, which are more and more frequent every year. I am perhaps misled by old age and fear, but I suspect that the human species – the *only* species – teeters at the verge of extinction, yet that the Library – enlightened, solitary, infinite, perfectly unmoving, armed with precious volumes, pointless, incorruptible, and secret – will endure.

I have just written the word 'infinite.' I have not included that adjective out of mere rhetorical habit; I hereby state that it is not illogical to think that the world is infinite. Those who believe it to have limits hypothesize that in some remote place or places the corridors and staircases and hexagons may, inconceivably, end – which is absurd. And yet those who picture the world as unlimited forget that the number of possible books is *not*. I will be bold enough to suggest this solution to the ancient problem: *The Library is unlimited but periodic.* If an eternal traveler should journey in any direction, he would find after untold centuries that the same volumes are repeated in the same disorder – which, repeated, becomes order: the Order. My solitude is cheered by that elegant hope.*

Mar del Plata, 1941

---

* Letizia Alvarez de Toledo has observed that the vast Library is pointless; strictly speaking, all that is required is a *single volume*, of the common size, printed in nine- or ten-point type, that would consist of an infinite number of infinitely thin pages. (In the early seventeenth century, Cavalieri stated that every solid body is the superposition of an infinite number of planes.) Using that silken *vademecum* would not be easy: each apparent page would open into other similar pages; the inconceivable middle page would have no 'back.'

The Theme of the Traitor and the Hero

So the Platonic Year
Whirls out new right and wrong
Whirls in the old instead;
All men are dancers and their tread
Goes to the barbarous clangour of a gong.

W. B. Yeats, *The Tower*

Under the notorious influence of Chesterton (inventor and embellisher of elegant mysteries) and the court counselor Leibniz (who invented preestablished harmony), in my spare evenings I have conceived this plot – which I will perhaps commit to paper but which already somehow justifies me. It needs details, rectifications, tinkering – there are areas of the story that have never been revealed to me. Today, January 3, 1944, I see it in the following way:

The action takes place in an oppressed yet stubborn country – Poland, Ireland, the republic of Venice, some South American or Balkan state. . . . Or *took* place rather, for though the narrator is contemporary, the story told by him occurred in the mid or early nineteenth century – in 1824, let us say, for convenience's sake; in Ireland, let us also say. The narrator is a man named Ryan, the great-grandson of the young, heroic, beautiful, murdered

Fergus Kilpatrick, whose grave was mysteriously violated, whose name gives luster to Browning's and Hugo's verses, and whose statue stands high upon a gray hilltop among red bogs.

Kilpatrick was a conspirator and a secret and glorious captain of conspirators. Like Moses, who from the land of Moab glimpsed yet could not reach the promised land, Kilpatrick perished on the eve of the victorious rebellion he had planned for and dreamed of. The date of the first centenary of his death is approaching; the circumstances of the crime are enigmatic; Ryan, who is writing a biography of the hero, discovers that the enigma goes deeper than mere detective work can fathom. Kilpatrick was murdered in a theater; the English police never apprehended the assassin. Historians claim that this failure does not tarnish the good name of the police, since it is possible that the police themselves had Kilpatrick murdered. Other aspects of the mystery disturb Ryan; certain things seem almost cyclical, seem to repeat or combine events from distant places, distant ages. For example: Everyone knows that the constables who examined the hero's body found a sealed letter warning Kilpatrick not to go to the theater that night; Julius Caesar, too, as he was walking toward the place where the knives of his friends awaited him, received a note he never read – a note telling him of his betrayal and revealing the names of his betrayers. Caesar's wife, Calpurnia, saw in dreams a tower felled by order of the Senate; on the eve of Kilpatrick's death, false and anonymous rumors of the burning of the circular tower of Kilgarvan spread throughout the country – an event that might be taken as an omen, since Kilpatrick had been born in Kilgarvan. These (and other) parallels between the story of Julius Caesar and the story of an Irish conspirator induce Ryan to imagine some secret shape of time, a pattern of repeating lines. His thoughts turn to the decimal history conceived by Condorcet, the morphologies proposed by Hegel, Spengler, and Vico, mankind as posited by Hesiod, degenerating from gold to iron. He thinks of the transmigration of souls, a doctrine that lends horror to Celtic literature and that Caesar himself attributed to the Druids of Britain; he toys with the idea that before Fergus Kilpatrick was Fergus Kilpatrick, he was Julius Caesar. He is saved from those circular labyrinths by a curious discovery, a discovery which, however, will plunge him deep into other, yet more tangled and heterogeneous mazes: It seems that certain words spoken by a beggar who spoke with Fergus Kilpatrick on the day of his death had been prefigured by Shakespeare, in *Macbeth*. The idea that history might have copied history is mind-boggling enough; that history should copy *literature* is inconceivable. . . . Ryan digs further, and he finds that in 1814 James Alexander Nolan, the oldest of the hero's comrades, had translated Shakespeare's major plays into Gaelic – among them *Julius Caesar*. He also finds in the archives a manuscript article by Nolan on the Swiss *Festspiele* – vast peripatetic theatrical performances that require thousands of actors and retell historical episodes in the same cities, the same mountains in which they occurred. Another unpublished document reveals to Ryan that a few days before the end, Kilpatrick, presiding over the last gathering of his chiefs, had signed the death sentence of a traitor, whose name has been scratched out. This sentence does not jibe with Kilpatrick's customary mercifulness. Ryan investigates the matter (his investigation being one of the gaps in the book's narration) and manages to decipher the enigma.

Kilpatrick was murdered in a theater, yet the entire city played the role of theater, too, and the actors were legion, and the play that was crowned by Kilpatrick's death took place over many days and many nights. Here is what happened:

On August 2, 1824, the conspirators met. The country was ripe for rebellion; something, however, always went awry – there must have been a traitor within the inner circle. Fergus Kilpatrick had given James Nolan the job of ferreting out the identity of this traitor, and Nolan had carried out his mission. He announced to the gathered comrades that the traitor was Kilpatrick himself. He proved the truth of his accusation beyond the shadow of a doubt, and the men at the council that night condemned their leader to death. The leader signed his own death sentence, but he pleaded that his punishment not harm the cause.

And so it was that Nolan conceived a strange plan. Ireland idolized Kilpatrick; the slightest suspicion of his baseness would have compromised the rebellion; Nolan proposed a way to turn the traitor's execution into an instrument for the emancipation of the country. He proposed that the condemned man die at the hands of an unknown assassin in deliberately dramatic circumstances; those circumstances would engrave themselves upon the popular imagination and hasten the rebellion. Kilpatrick swore to collaborate in this plan which would give him an occasion to redeem himself, and which would be crowned by his death.

Nolan had no time to invent the circumstances of the multiple execution from scratch, and so he plagiarized the scene from another playwright, the English enemy Will Shakespeare, reprising scenes from *Macbeth* and *Julius Caesar*. The public yet secret performance occurred over several days. The condemned man entered Dublin, argued, worked, prayed, reprehended, spoke words of pathos – and each of those acts destined to shine forth in glory had been choreographed by Nolan. Hundreds of actors collaborated with the protagonist; the role of some was complex, the role of others a matter of moments on the stage. The things they did and said endure in Ireland's history books and in its impassioned memory. Kilpatrick, moved almost to ecstasy by the scrupulously plotted fate that would redeem him and end his days, more than once enriched his judge's text with improvised words and acts. Thus the teeming drama played itself out in time, until that August 6, 1824, in a box (prefiguring Lincoln's) draped with funereal curtains, when a yearned-for bullet pierced the traitor-hero's breast. Between two spurts of sudden blood, Kilpatrick could hardly pronounce the few words given him to speak.

In Nolan's play, the passages taken from Shakespeare are the *least* dramatic ones; Ryan suspected that the author interpolated them so that someone, in the future, would be able to stumble upon the truth. Ryan realized that he, too, was part of Nolan's plot. . . . After long and stubborn deliberation, he decided to silence the discovery. He published a book dedicated to the hero's glory; that too, perhaps, had been foreseen.

The Witness

In a stable that stands almost in the shadow of the new stone church, a man with gray eyes and gray beard, lying amid the odor of the animals, humbly tries to will himself into death, much as a man might will himself to sleep. The day, obedient to vast and secret laws, slowly shifts about and mingles the shadows in the lowly place; outside lie plowed fields, a ditch clogged with dead leaves, and the faint track of a wolf in the black clay where the line of woods begins. The man sleeps and dreams, forgotten. The bells for orisons awaken him. Bells are now one of evening's customs in the kingdoms of England, but as a boy the man has seen the face of Woden, the sacred horror and the exultation, the clumsy wooden idol laden with Roman coins and ponderous vestments, the sacrifice of horses, dogs, and prisoners. Before dawn he will be dead, and with him, the last eyewitness images of pagan rites will perish, never to be seen again. The world will be a little poorer when this Saxon man is dead.

Things, events, that occupy space yet come to an end when someone dies may make us stop in wonder – and yet one thing, or an infinite number of things, dies with every man's or woman's death, unless the universe itself has a memory, as theosophists have suggested. In the course of time there was one day that closed the last eyes that had looked on Christ; the Battle of Junín and the love of Helen died with the death of one man. What will die with me the day I die? What pathetic or frail image will be lost to the world? The voice of Macedonio Fernández, the image of a bay horse in a vacant lot on the corner of Sarrano and Charcas, a bar of sulfur in the drawer of a mahogany desk?

Ragnarök

The images in dreams, wrote Coleridge, figure forth the impressions that our intellect would call causes; we do not feel horror because we are haunted by a sphinx, we dream a sphinx in order to explain the horror that we feel. If that is true, how might a mere chronicling of its forms transmit the stupor, the exultation, the alarms, the dread, and the joy that wove together that night's dream? I shall attempt that chronicle, nonetheless; perhaps the fact that the dream consisted of but a single scene may erase or soften the essential difficulty.

The place was the College of Philosophy and Letters; the hour, nightfall. Everything (as is often the case in dreams) was slightly different; a slight magnification altered things. We chose authorities; I would speak with Pedro Henríquez Ureña,* who in waking life had

* Pedro Henríquez Ureña (1884–1946), originally from the Dominican Republic, lived for years in Buenos Aires and was an early contributor to *Sur*, the magazine that Victoria Ocampo founded and that JLB assiduously worked on. It was through Henríquez Ureña, who had lived for a time in Mexico City, that JLB met another friend, the Mexican humanist Alfonso Reyes. Henríquez Ureña and JLB collaborated on the *Antología de la literatura argentina* (1937), and they were very close friends.

died many years before. Suddenly, we were dumb-founded by a great noise of demonstrators or street musicians. From the Underworld, we heard the cries of humans and animals. A voice cried: *Here they come!* and then: *The gods! the gods!* Four or five individuals emerged from out of the mob and occupied the dais of the auditorium. Everyone applauded, weeping; it was the gods, returning after a banishment of many centuries. Looming larger than life as they stood upon the dais, their heads thrown back and their chests thrust forward, they haughtily received our homage. One of them was holding a branch (which belonged, no doubt, to the simple botany of dreams); another, with a sweeping gesture, held out a hand that was a claw; one of Janus' faces looked mistrustfully at Thoth's curved beak. Perhaps excited by our applause, one of them, I no longer remember which, burst out in a triumphant, incredibly bitter clucking that was half gargle and half whistle. From that point on, things changed.

It all began with the suspicion (perhaps exaggerated) that the gods were unable to talk. Centuries of a feral life of flight had atrophied that part of them that was human; the moon of Islam and the cross of Rome had been implacable with these fugitives. Beetling brows, yellowed teeth, the sparse beard of a mulatto or a Chinaman, and beastlike dewlaps were testaments to the degeneration of the Olympian line. The clothes they wore were not those of a decorous and honest poverty, but rather of the criminal luxury of the Underworld's gambling dens and houses of ill repute. A carnation bled from a buttonhole; under a tight suitcoat one could discern the outline of a knife. Suddenly, we felt that they were playing their last trump, that they were cunning, ignorant, and cruel, like aged predators, and that if we allowed ourselves to be swayed by fear or pity, they would wind up destroying us.

We drew our heavy revolvers (suddenly in the dream there were revolvers) and exultantly killed the gods.

Blue Tigers

A famous poem by Blake paints the tiger as a fire burning bright and an eternal archetype of Evil; I prefer the Chesterton maxim that casts the tiger as a symbol of terrible elegance. Apart from these, there are no words that can rune the tiger, that shape which for centuries has lived in the imagination of mankind. I have always been drawn to the tiger. I know that as a boy I would linger before one particular cage at the zoo; the others held no interest for me. I would judge encyclopedias and natural histories by their engravings of the tiger. When the *Jungle Books* were revealed to me I was upset that the tiger, Shere Khan, was the hero's enemy. As the years passed, this strange fascination never left me; it survived my paradoxical desire to become a hunter as it did all common human vicissitudes. Until not long ago (the date feels distant but it really is not), it coexisted peacefully with my day-to-day labors at the University of Lahore. I am a professor of Eastern and Western logic, and I consecrate my Sundays to a seminar on the philosophy of Spinoza. I should add that I am a Scotsman; it may have been my love of tigers that brought me from Aberdeen to Punjab. The outward course of my life has been the common one, but in my dreams I always saw tigers. Now it is other forms that fill them.

I have recounted all these facts more than once, until now they seem almost to belong to someone else. I let them stand, however, since they are required by my statement.

Toward the end of 1904, I read that in the region of the Ganges delta a blue variety of the species had been discovered. The news was confirmed by subsequent telegrams, with the contradictions and incongruities that one expects in such cases. My old love stirred once more. Nevertheless, I suspected some error, since the names of colors are notoriously imprecise. I remembered having once read that in Icelandic, Ethiopia was 'Blaland,' Blue Land *or* the Land of Black Men. The blue tiger might well be a black panther. Nothing was mentioned of stripes; the picture published by the London press, showing a blue tiger with silver stripes, was patently apocryphal. Similarly, the blue of the illustration looked more like that of heraldry than reality. In a dream, I saw tigers of a blue I had never seen before, and for which I could find no word. I know it was almost black, but that description of course does scant justice to the shade I saw.

Some months later, a colleague of mine told me that in a certain village miles from the Ganges he had heard talk of blue tigers. I was astonished by that piece of news, because tigers are rare in that area. Once again I dreamed of the blue tiger, throwing its long shadow as it made its way over the sandy ground. I took advantage of the end of term to make a journey to that village, whose name (for reasons that will soon be clear) I do not wish to recall.

I arrived toward the end of the rainy season. The village squatted at the foot of a hill (which looked to me wider than it was high) and was surrounded and menaced by the jungle, which was a dark brown color. Surely one of the pages of Kipling contains that village of my adventure, since all of India, all the world somehow, can be found there. Suffice it to report that a ditch, and swaying cane-stalk bridges, constituted the huts' fragile defense. Toward the south there were swamps and rice fields and a ravine with a muddy river whose name I never learned, and beyond that, again, the jungle.

The people who lived in the village were Hindus. I did not like this, though I had foreseen it. I have always gotten along better with Muslims, though Islam, I know, is the poorest of the religions that spring from Judaism.

We feel ordinarily that India teems with humanity; in the village I felt that India teemed with *jungle*. It crept virtually into the huts. The days were oppressive, and the nights brought no relief.

I was greeted upon my arrival by the elders, with whom I sustained a tentative conversation constructed of vague courtesies. I have mentioned the poverty of the place, but I know that it is an axiom of every man's belief that the land he lives in and owes his allegiance to possesses some unique distinction, and so I praised in glowing terms the dubious habitations and the no less dubious delicacies served me, and I declared that the fame of that region had reached Lahore. The expressions on the men's faces changed; I immediately sensed that I had committed a *faux pas* I might come to regret. I sensed that these people possessed a secret they would not share with a stranger. Perhaps they worshiped the blue tiger, perhaps they were devotees of a cult that my rash words had profaned.

I waited until the next morning. When the rice had been consumed and the tea drunk down, I broached my subject. Despite the previous night's experience, I did not understand – was incapable of understanding – what took place then. The entire village looked at me with stupefaction, almost with terror, but when I told them that my purpose was to capture the beast with the curious skin, they seemed almost relieved at my words. One of them said he had seen the animal at the edge of the jungle.

In the middle of the night, they woke me. A boy told me that a goat had escaped from the corral and that as he'd gone to look for it, he'd seen the blue tiger on the far bank of the river. I reflected that the scant light of the new moon would hardly have allowed him to make out the color, but everyone confirmed the tale; one of them, who had been silent up until that moment, said he had seen it, too. We went out with the rifles and I saw, or thought I saw, a feline shadow slink into the shadows of the jungle. They did not find the goat, but the creature that had taken it might or might not have been my blue tiger. They emphatically pointed out to me other traces – which of course proved nothing.

After a few nights I realized that these false alarms

were a sort of routine. Like Daniel Defoe, the men of the village were skilled at inventing circumstantial details. The tiger might be glimpsed at any hour, out toward the rice fields to the south or up toward the jungle to the north, but it did not take me long to realize that there was a suspicious regularity in the way the villagers seemed to take turns spotting it. My arrival upon the scene of the sighting invariably coincided with the precise instant that the tiger had just run off. I was always shown a trail, a paw mark, some broken twig, but a man's fist can counterfeit a tiger's prints. Once or twice I witnessed a dead dog. One moonlit night we staked out a goat as a lure, but we watched fruitlessly until dawn. I thought at first that these daily fables were meant to encourage me to prolong my stay, for it did benefit the village – the people sold me food and did domestic chores for me. To verify this conjecture, I told them that I was thinking of moving on to another region, downstream, in quest of the tiger. I was surprised to find that they welcomed my decision. I continued to sense, however, that there was a secret, and that everyone was keeping a wary eye on me.

I mentioned earlier that the wooded hill at whose foot the village sprawled was not really very high; it was flat on top, a sort of plateau. On the other side of the mountain, toward the west and north, the jungle began again. Since the slope was not a rugged one, one afternoon I suggested that we climb it. My simple words threw the villagers into consternation. One exclaimed that the mountainside was too steep. The eldest of them said gravely that my goal was impossible to attain, the summit of the hill was sacred, magical obstacles blocked the ascent to man. He who trod the peak with mortal foot was in danger of seeing the godhead, and of going blind or mad.

I did not argue, but that night, when everyone was asleep, I stole soundlessly from my hut and began to climb the easy hillside.

There was no path, and the undergrowth held me back. The moon was just at the horizon. I took note of everything with singular attentiveness, as though I sensed that this was to be an important day, perhaps the most important day of all my days. I still recall the dark, almost black, shadings of the leaves and bushes. It was close to dawn, and the sky was beginning to turn pale, but in all the jungle around, not one bird sang.

Twenty or thirty minutes' climb brought me to the summit. It took me very little effort to imagine that it was cooler there than in the village, which sweltered down below. I had been right that this was not a peak, but rather a plateau, a sort of terrace, not very broad, and that the jungle crept up to it all around, on the flanks of the hill. I felt free, as though my residence in the village had been a prison. I didn't care that the villagers had tried to fool me; I felt they were somehow children.

As for the tiger . . . Constant frustration had exhausted my curiosity and my faith, but almost mechanically I looked for tracks.

The ground was cracked and sandy. In one of the

cracks – which by the way were not deep, and which branched into others – I caught a glimpse of a color. Incredibly, it was the same color as the tiger of my dreams. I wish I had never laid eyes on it. I looked closely. The crevice was full of little stones, all alike, circular, just a few centimeters in diameter and very smooth. Their regularity lent them an air almost of artificiality, as though they were coins, or buttons, or counters in some game.

I bent down, put my hand into the crevice, and picked out some of the stones. I felt a faint quivering. I put the handful of little stones in the right pocket of my jacket, where there were a small pair of scissors and a letter from Allahabad. Those two chance objects have their place in my story.

Back in my hut, I took off my jacket. I lay down and dreamed once more of the tiger. In my dream I took special note of its color; it was the color of the tiger I had dreamed of, and also of the little stones from the plateau. The late-morning sun in my face woke me. I got up. The scissors and the letter made it hard to take the disks out of the pocket; they kept getting in the way. I pulled out a handful, but felt that there were still two or three I had missed. A tickling sensation, the slightest sort of quivering, imparted a soft warmth to my palm. When I opened my hand, I saw that it held thirty or forty disks; I'd have sworn I'd picked up no more than ten. I left them on the table and turned back to get the rest out of the pocket. I didn't need to count them to see that they had multiplied. I pushed them together into a single pile, and tried to count them out one by one.

That simple operation turned out to be impossible. I would look fixedly at any one of them, pick it up with my thumb and index finger, yet when I had done that, when that one disk was separated from the rest, it would have become many. I checked to see that I didn't have a fever (which I did not), and then I performed the same experiment, over and over again. The obscene miracle kept happening. I felt my feet go clammy and my bowels turn to ice; my knees began to shake. I do not know how much time passed.

Without looking at the disks, I scooped them into a pile and threw them out the window. With a strange feeling of relief, I sensed that their number had dwindled. I firmly closed the door and lay down on my bed. I tried to find the exact position I had been lying in before, hoping to persuade myself that all this had been a dream. So as not to think about the disks yet somehow fill the time, I repeated, with slow precision, aloud, the eight definitions and seven axioms of Ethics. I am not sure they helped.

In the midst of these exorcistic exercises, a knock came at my door. Instinctively fearing that I had been overheard talking to myself, I went to the door and opened it.

It was the headman of the village, Bhagwan Dass. For a second his presence seemed to restore me to every-day reality. We stepped outside. I harbored some hope that the disks might have disappeared, but there they were, on the ground. I no longer can be sure how many there were.

The elder looked down at them and then looked at me.

'These stones are not from here. They are stones from up there,' he said, in a voice that was not his own.

'That's true,' I replied. I added, not without some defiance, that I had found them up on the plateau, but I was immediately ashamed of myself for feeling that I owed anyone an explanation. Bhagwan Dass ignored me; he continued to stare in fascination at the stones. I ordered him to pick them up. He did not move.

I am grieved to admit that I took out my revolver and repeated the order, this time in a somewhat more forceful tone of voice.

'A bullet in the breast is preferable to a blue stone in the hand,' stammered Bhagwan Dass.

'You are a coward,' said I.

I was, I believe, no less terrified than he, but I closed my eyes and picked up a handful of stones with my left hand. I tucked the pistol in my belt and dropped the stones one by one into the open palm of my right hand. Their number had grown considerably.

I had unwittingly become accustomed to those transformations. They now surprised me less than Bhagwan Dass' cries.

'These are the stones that spawn!' he exclaimed. 'There are many of them now, but they can change. Their shape is that of the moon when it is full, and their color is the blue that we are permitted to see only in our dreams. My father's father spoke the truth when he told men of their power.'

The entire village crowded around us.

I felt myself to be the magical possessor of those wondrous objects. To the astonishment of all, I picked up the disks, raised them high, dropped them, scattered them, watched them grow and multiply or mysteriously dwindle.

The villagers huddled together, seized with astonishment and horror. Men forced their wives to look upon the wonder. One woman covered her face with her forearm, another squeezed her eyes shut tight. No one had the courage to touch the disks – save one happy boy-child that played with them. Just at that moment I sensed that all this confusion was profaning the miracle. I gathered the disks, all of them I could, and returned to my hut.

It may be that I have tried to forget the rest of that day, which was the first of a misfortunate series that continues even until now. Whether I tried to forget the day or not, I do not remember it. Toward evening, I began to think back on the night before, which had not been a particularly happy one, with a sort of nostalgia; at least it, like so many others, had been filled with my obsession with the tiger. I tried to find solace in that image once charged with power, now trivial. The blue tiger seemed no less innocuous than the Roman's black swan, which was discovered subsequently in Australia.

Rereading what I have written, I see that I have committed a fundamental error. Led astray by the habit of that good or bad literature wrongly called psychology, I have attempted to recover – I don't know why – the linear chronology of my find. Instead, I should have stressed the monstrousness of the disks.

If someone were to tell me that there are unicorns on the moon, I could accept or reject the report, or suspend judgment, but it is something I could imagine. If, on the other hand, I were told that six or seven unicorns on the moon could be three, I would declare *a priori* that such a thing was impossible. The man who has learned that three plus one are four doesn't have to go through a proof of that assertion with coins, or dice, or chess pieces, or pencils. He knows it, and that's that. He cannot conceive a different sum. There are mathematicians who say that three plus one is a *tautology* for four, a *different way of saying* 'four' . . . But I, Alexander Craigie, of all men on earth, was fated to discover the only objects that contradict that essential law of the human mind.

At first I was in a sort of agony, fearing that I'd gone mad; since then, I have come to believe that it would have been better had I been merely insane, for my personal hallucinations would be less disturbing than the discovery that the universe can tolerate disorder. If three plus one can be two, or fourteen, then reason is madness.

During that time, I often dreamed about the stones. The fact that the dream did not recur every night left me a sliver of hope, though a hope that soon turned to terror. The dream was always more or less the same;

the beginning heralded the feared end. A spiral staircase – an iron railing and a few iron treads – and then a cellar, or system of cellars, leading through the depths to other stairways that might abruptly end, or suddenly lead into ironworks, locksmith's forges, dungeons, or swamps. At the bottom, in their expected crevice in the earth, the stones, which were also Behemoth, or Leviathan – the creatures of the Scriptures that signify that God is irrational. I would awaken trembling, and there the stones would be, in their box, ready to transform themselves.

The villagers' attitude toward me began to change. I had been touched by something of the divinity that inhered in the stones the villagers had named 'blue tigers,' but I was also known to have profaned the summit. At any moment of the night, at any moment of the day, the gods might punish me. The villagers dared not attack me or condemn what I had done, but I noticed that everyone was now dangerously servile. I never again laid eyes on the child who had played with the stones. I feared poison, or a knife in the back. One morning before dawn I slipped out of the village. I sensed that its entire population had been keeping an eye on me, and that my escape would be a relief to them. Since that first morning, no one had ever asked to see the stones.

I returned to Lahore, the handful of disks in my pocket. The familiar environment of my books did not bring the relief I sought. That abominable village, and the jungle, and the jungle's thorny slope rising to the plateau, and on the plateau the little crevices, and within the crevices, the stones – all that, I felt, continued to exist on the planet. My dreams confused and multiplied those dissimilar things. The village was the stones, the jungle was the swamp, the swamp was the jungle.

I shunned the company of my friends. I feared that I would yield to the temptation of showing them that dreadful miracle that undermined humanity's science.

I performed several experiments. I made a cross-shaped incision in one of the disks, put that disk with the others, and shuffled them around; within one or two conversions, I had lost it, though the number of disks had increased. I performed an analogous test with a disk from which I filed a semicircular notch. That disk also disappeared. I punched a hole in the center of one disk with an awl and tried the test again. That disk disappeared forever. The next day the disk with the cross cut in it reappeared from its journey into the void. What mysterious sort of space was this, which in obedience to inscrutable laws or some inhuman will absorbed the stones and then in time threw an occasional one back again?

The same yearning for order that had created mathematics in the first place made me seek some order in that aberration of mathematics, the insensate stones that propagate themselves. I attempted to find a law within their unpredictable variations. I devoted days and nights alike to establishing statistics on the changes. From that stage of my investigations I still have several notebooks, vainly filled with ciphers. My procedure was this: I would count the stones by eye and write down the figure. Then I would divide them into two handfuls that I would scatter separately on the table. I would count the two totals, note them down, and repeat the operation. This search for order, for a secret design within the rotations, led nowhere. The largest number of stones I counted was 419; the smallest, three. There was a moment when I hoped, or feared, that they would disappear altogether. It took little experimenting to show that one of the disks, isolated from the others, could not multiply or disappear.

Naturally, the four mathematical operations – adding, subtracting, multiplying, and dividing – were impossible. The stones resisted arithmetic as they did the calculation of probability. Forty disks, divided, might become nine; those nine in turn divided might yield three hundred. I do not know how much they weighed. I did not have recourse to a scale, but I am sure that their weight was constant, and light. Their color was always that same blue.

These operations helped save me from madness. As I manipulated the stones that destroyed the science of mathematics, more than once I thought of those Greek stones that were the first ciphers and that had been passed down to so many languages as the word 'calculus.' Mathematics, I told myself, had its origin, and now has its end, in stones. If Pythagoras had worked with these . . .

After about a month I realized that there was no way out of the chaos. There lay the unruly disks, there lay the constant temptation to touch them, to feel that tickling sensation once more, to scatter them, to watch them increase or decrease, and to note whether they came out odd or even. I came to fear that they would contaminate other things – particularly the fingers that insisted upon handling them.

For several days I imposed upon myself the private obligation to think continually about the stones, because I knew that forgetting them was possible only for a moment, and that rediscovering my torment would be unbearable.

I did not sleep the night of February 10. After a walk that led me far into the dawn, I passed through the gates of the mosque of Wazil Khan. It was the hour at which light has not yet revealed the colors of things. There was not a soul in the courtyard. Not knowing why, I plunged my hands into the water of the fountain of ablutions. Inside the mosque, it occurred to me that God and Allah are two names for a single, inconceivable Being, and I prayed aloud that I be freed from my burden. Unmoving, I awaited some reply.

I heard no steps, but a voice, quite close, spoke to me:

'I am here.'

A beggar was standing beside me. In the soft light I could make out his turban, his sightless eyes, his sallow skin, his gray beard. He was not very tall.

He put out a hand to me, and said, still softly:

'Alms, oh Protector of the Poor . . .'

I put my hands in my pockets.

'I have not a single coin,' I replied.

'You have many,' was the beggar's answer.

The stones were in my right pocket. I took out one and dropped it into his cupped palm. There was not the slightest sound.

'You must give me all of them,' he said. 'He who gives not all has given nothing.'

I understood, and I said:

'I want you to know that my alms may be a curse.'

'Perhaps that gift is the only gift I am permitted to receive. I have sinned.'

I dropped all the stones into the concave hand. They fell as though into the bottom of the sea, without the slightest whisper.

Then the man spoke again:

'I do not yet know what your gift to me is, but mine to you is an awesome one. You may keep your days and nights, and keep wisdom, habits, the world.'

I did not hear the blind beggar's steps, or see him disappear into the dawn.

POCKET PENGUINS

POCKET PENGUINS